The Jewel Fairies

For Danni who loves fairies

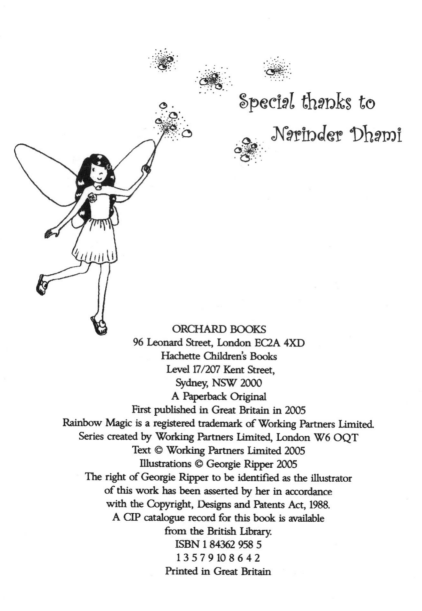

Special thanks to
Narinder Dhami

ORCHARD BOOKS
96 Leonard Street, London EC2A 4XD
Hachette Children's Books
Level 17/207 Kent Street,
Sydney, NSW 2000
A Paperback Original
First published in Great Britain in 2005
Rainbow Magic is a registered trademark of Working Partners Limited.
Series created by Working Partners Limited, London W6 OQT
Text © Working Partners Limited 2005
Illustrations © Georgie Ripper 2005
The right of Georgie Ripper to be identified as the illustrator
of this work has been asserted by her in accordance
with the Copyright, Designs and Patents Act, 1988.
A CIP catalogue record for this book is available
from the British Library.
ISBN 1 84362 958 5
1 3 5 7 9 10 8 6 4 2
Printed in Great Britain

India
the Moonstone
Fairy

by Daisy Meadows

illustrated by Georgie Ripper

ORCHARD BOOKS

www.rainbowmagic.co.uk

The Fairyland Palace

Adventure Playground

Tippington Manor

Tippington Town

The Tall Toy Store

Fountain

By Frosty magic I cast away
These seven jewels with their fiery rays,
So their magic powers will not be felt
And my icy castle shall not melt.

The fairies may search high and low
To find the gems and take them home.
But I will send my goblin guards
To make the fairies' mission hard.

Contents

A Nasty Nightmare

"Kirsty, help!" Rachel Walker shouted.
"The goblins are going to get me!"

Panting, Rachel glanced behind her.
She was running as fast as she could,
but the green goblins were getting closer
and closer. They were grinning nastily,
showing their pointed teeth. Now one
of them had grabbed Rachel by the

shoulder, and was shaking her hard—

"Rachel?" Kirsty Tate was leaning over her friend's bed, shaking her awake. "Wake up! You're having a nightmare."

Rachel woke and sat up in bed. "What time is it?" she asked. "I dreamt that there were horrible goblins chasing me, and I couldn't escape."

"It's 7.30," Kirsty replied, perching on the edge of the bed. "Why were the goblins after you?"

Rachel frowned. "I can't remember," she sighed. "But you know what, Kirsty? I've got a funny feeling that Jack Frost might be up to something again!"

Kirsty's eyes opened wide. "Oh, do you really think so?" she gasped. "Then maybe our fairy friends will need our help!"

Rachel and Kirsty shared a magical secret. They had become friends with the fairies, and whenever there was a problem in Fairyland, Kirsty and Rachel were called on to help.

The fairies' greatest enemy was Jack Frost. He was always looking for ways to make trouble, helped by his mean goblin servants. Not long ago, Jack Frost had tried to ruin the celebration party for King Oberon and Queen Titania's 1000th jubilee. But luckily, Kirsty and Rachel had come to the rescue.

"We'll have to keep our eyes open," Rachel agreed. "If the fairies need our help, they'll let us know somehow."

Kirsty nodded. "Well, it's only the beginning of half-term, and I'm staying with you for the whole week," she pointed out. "So we have plenty of time."

Before Rachel could reply, the sweet, tinkling sound of music suddenly filled the room. Both Kirsty and Rachel jumped.

"What's that?" Kirsty asked.

Rachel looked puzzled for a moment, but then she began to laugh. "It's my music box!" she smiled, pointing at the dressing-table. "The one the Party Fairies gave us."

After helping the Party Fairies to stop Jack Frost from spoiling the jubilee celebrations, Rachel and Kirsty had each been given a beautiful, musical jewellery box with a tiny fairy on top. Rachel's box sat on her dressing-table, and the girls could see that the fairy was spinning round in time to the music.

"Yes, but how did it start up on its own?" Kirsty asked, with a frown. "I didn't wind it, and you've only just woken up."

"Look!" Rachel gasped. "The box is glowing!"

Rachel scrambled out of bed, and she and Kirsty rushed over to take a closer look. Rachel was right. The box was glowing with a faint pink light which shone from under the closed lid.

"Lift the lid, Rachel," Kirsty whispered.

Hardly daring to breathe, Rachel reached out and slowly lifted the lid.

Immediately a glittering shower of multi-coloured fairy dust burst from the jewellery box. It swirled around the girls, wrapping them in a cloud of sparkles and lifting them off their feet.

Fairy News

After just a moment or two, the sparkles began to drift away and the girls felt their feet lightly touch the ground. Rachel and Kirsty blinked a few times and looked around.

"Kirsty, we're in Fairyland!" Rachel gasped.

"In our pyjamas!" Kirsty added.

The girls were now fairy-sized with glittering fairy wings on their backs, and they were standing in the golden Great Hall of the fairy palace. King Oberon, Queen Titania and a small crowd of fairies stood in front of them. The girls noticed that they all looked worried.

Queen Titania stepped forwards. "You are very welcome, girls," she said with a smile. "I hope you don't mind us bringing you here so unexpectedly."

"Of course not," Rachel said quickly.

"You have been such good friends to us in the past," the Queen went on, "that we were hoping we could call on you again, now that we are in trouble."

"What's wrong?" asked Kirsty anxiously.

"Let me explain," the Queen replied sadly. "Every year, at Halloween, we have a huge celebration in Fairyland. All the fairies have to recharge their fairy magic for another year."

"So every fairy in Fairyland parades around the Grand Square," King Oberon put in. "Then they all march into the palace to a very special chamber, where Queen Titania's tiara rests upon a velvet cushion."

"It sounds wonderful," Rachel sighed, hoping that she and Kirsty might be allowed to watch the grand procession one day.

Queen Titania nodded. "It is," she replied. "And my tiara is very important for fairy magic. It has seven beautiful jewels set in it. A sparkling fountain of fairy dust pours from each of the seven jewels, and they join together to form one great, glittering rainbow of magical fairy dust."

Kirsty and Rachel were listening carefully, their eyes wide.

"What happens then?" Kirsty asked.

"Each fairy must dip her wand in the rainbow fountain to recharge it," the Queen explained. "Then she will be able to perform magic for another year."

The King shook his head sadly. "But now Jack Frost has put a stop to all that," he sighed. "Two nights ago, he crept into the palace and stole the seven jewels from the Queen's tiara!"

"Oh, no!" Rachel and Kirsty exclaimed together.

"Our special celebration was to take place in a week's time," the Queen went on, looking worried. "So the fairies' magic is already running low."

"The jewels must be returned to the tiara," King Oberon added, "before the fairies run out of the jewels' magic completely!"

"Does this mean that there will be no

magic at all left in Fairyland?" asked Kirsty anxiously.

"Not exactly," the Queen replied. "Fairy magic isn't quite as simple as that. Some magic, like Weather Magic and Rainbow Magic, aren't controlled by by the jewels."

"But the jewels do control some of the most important kinds of fairy magic," the King explained. "Like flying, wishes and sweet dreams. Some people have already started to have nightmares."

Rachel nodded, thinking of her own scary dream. "We have to get the jewels back!" she said firmly.

"Where is Jack Frost now?" Kirsty wanted to know. "Has he taken the jewels to his ice castle?"

The Queen shook her head. "Jack Frost doesn't have the jewels any more," she said. "Come with me, and I will show you what happened."

Rachel and Kirsty followed the fairies outside into the beautiful palace gardens. They stopped beside the golden pool, its surface as clear and smooth as glass.

"Look," Queen Titania said softly, waving her wand over the water.

Immediately tiny ripples began to spread across the surface of the pool. The ripples grew bigger and bigger, and slowly a picture appeared on the water's surface.

"It's Jack Frost!" Rachel exclaimed.
Tall, thin, spiky Jack Frost stood
in front of Queen Titania's
golden tiara upon its
velvet cushion. The
seven magic jewels
glittered as dazzling
streams of magic
dust poured
from each one.
Laughing, Jack
Frost thrust his
snowflake-tipped
wand into the
magic rainbow
fountain, where it
glowed like fire.
"He is recharging his
magic," the King explained.

Kirsty and Rachel watched in dismay as Jack Frost then prised the sparkling gems from the golden tiara. He waved his wand and immediately the jewels were encased in solid ice.

"What is he doing?" Rachel asked, puzzled.

"The light and heat of the jewels' magic makes them difficult for cold, icy creatures like Jack Frost and his goblins to hold," Queen Titania explained. "Look."

Now Jack Frost was whizzing back to his ice castle, carried by a frosty wind which blew him along. He carried the jewels in his arms, but Rachel and Kirsty could see that the hard shell of frost around them was already beginning to melt.

Jack Frost swooped down from the grey
sky and landed in the throne room of his
ice castle. By this time the frost around
the jewels had almost melted away. The
jewels glowed, casting shimmering rays of
light like laser beams into every corner of
the icy room. Goblins came running to
see the gems, wearing sunglasses to protect
their eyes from the glare.

"Stand back, you fools!" Jack Frost
roared, waving his wand again and

casting another spell to cover the jewels with ice. But the jewels were still glowing, and the ice began to melt away almost immediately.

"Look, master," yelled one of the goblins suddenly, "the fairy magic is melting your castle!"

Jack Frost looked round in a fury. Sure enough, water was beginning to trickle down the icy walls, and there was a puddle at the foot of his throne.

"Jack Frost's magic is not strong enough to block the power of the jewels," Queen Titania told Rachel and Kirsty.

The girls watched as the goblins began rushing around, mopping up the water as fast as they could. But as quickly as they cleared one puddle away, two more appeared.

"Very well then," shouted Jack Frost, stamping his feet in rage. "If I cannot keep these magic jewels, no one else shall have them! I will cast a spell to get rid of them." And he raised his wand high above his head.

Lost!

"Oh, no!" Kirsty gasped. She and Rachel watched in horror as an icy blast of wind whipped up around the throne room. The glowing jewels were sent spinning and tumbling across the room and out of the window, where they scattered far and wide.

"See how the jewels grow larger as they fall into the human world?" Queen Titania pointed out, just as the picture in the pool began to flicker and fade. "Because they are magical, they'll hide themselves until we can find them and bring them back to Fairyland."

The picture in the pool was fading fast. But just before it disappeared,

Rachel saw one of the jewels,
a creamy-coloured stone,
fall into someone's
back garden. With
a start of surprise,
Rachel realised that
she knew exactly
whose garden it was!

The Queen was shaking
her head sadly as the picture vanished
completely. "All of our fairy seeing
magic is used up," she sighed. "So the
pool can't show us where all the jewels
have gone."

"But I know where one of them is!"
Rachel burst out excitedly. "I recognised
the garden where it fell!"

Everyone turned to stare at her.

"Are you sure, Rachel?" Kirsty asked.

Rachel nodded. "It was Mr and Mrs Palmer's back garden," she explained. "The Palmers are friends of my parents, and I've been to their house loads of times to help Mum babysit their little girl, Ellie."

One of the fairies was so excited at this that she whirled up into the air, her long brown hair streaming out behind her. "I'm India, the Moonstone Fairy," she cried, her eyes shining. "And I'm sure it was my Moonstone which fell into your friends' back garden!"

The little fairy wore a pretty dress with a nipped-in waist and floaty skirt.

The dress was white, but every time India moved, flashes of shimmering pink and blue shot through the material. On her feet she wore dainty white sandals.

"You must meet all our Jewel Fairies," said King Oberon, as the other fairies crowded around. "Each one is responsible for teaching all the other fairies how to use her jewel's magic." He pointed at India the Moonstone Fairy. "India teaches dream magic, while Emily the Emerald Fairy teaches seeing magic, Scarlett the Garnet Fairy teaches growing and shrinking magic, Chloe the Topaz Fairy teaches changing magic, Sophie the Sapphire Fairy teaches wishing magic, Amy the Amethyst Fairy teaches appearing and disappearing magic, and Lucy the Diamond Fairy teaches flying magic."

Rachel and Kirsty smiled round at all the fairies.

"We'll do our best to get your jewels back," Kirsty said.

"Thank you," the fairies replied.

"We knew you would help us," Queen Titania said gratefully. "But Jack Frost knows we will be trying to find the jewels, and he has sent his goblins into the human world to guard them."

"The goblins will find it difficult to pick the jewels up," King Oberon went on. "The bright light and magic of the gems will burn them, because they belong to the cold, icy world of Jack Frost. Instead, the goblins will probably lurk near the jewels and try to stop us getting them back."

Rachel and Kirsty nodded thoughtfully.

Queen Titania looked grave. "So now we need your help not only to find each magic jewel," she finished, "but also to outwit the goblins that will be guarding them!"

On the Right Track

"We'll find a way to get the jewels back," Rachel said firmly, and Kirsty nodded.

King Oberon smiled at them. "And you will have our Jewel Fairies to help you."

Rachel frowned. "I had a dream about the goblins chasing me," she said slowly.

India sighed, looking
very sad. "Without
the Moonstone, the
fairies' power to
send sweet dreams
into the human
world is fading," she
explained. "That's why
you had a nightmare, Rachel."

"India will return with you to your
world," said Queen Titania. "She'll
help you find the Moonstone."

"We know we have to look in the
Palmers' back garden," Kirsty said.
"But how will we know where to
search for the other jewels?"

Queen Titania smiled. "Just as before,
you must let the magic come to you,"
she replied. "The jewels will find you.

And remember, they have grown bigger in the human world, so they will be easier to spot."

Rachel and Kirsty nodded. Then India fluttered over to join them and the Fairy Queen raised her wand.

"Good luck!" called the fairies, as the Queen waved her wand and Rachel, Kirsty and India disappeared in a shower of magic sparkles.

When the cloud of fairy dust vanished, Rachel and Kirsty realised that they were back in Rachel's bedroom.

"We must get to work right away, girls!" called a silvery voice.

The girls turned and saw India perched on the dressing-table mirror.

"Yes, let's go over to the Palmers' house now," said Rachel eagerly, making for the door.

Kirsty burst out laughing. "I think we'd better change out of our pyjamas first, don't you?"

"Good idea!" Rachel grinned.

"How can we get into the Palmers' back garden?" India asked, as the girls quickly got dressed.

"We could throw a ball over the fence," Kirsty suggested. "Then we could ask the Palmers if we can pop into their garden to find it."

"Yes, that would work," Rachel agreed.

"Girls, are you awake?" Mrs Walker's voice drifted up the stairs. "Breakfast's ready."

India fluttered across the room and hid

herself in Kirsty's pocket, and the girls hurried downstairs. "Mum," said Rachel, as she and Kirsty ate toast and jam, "is it OK if we go out to play after breakfast?"

"Yes," Mrs Walker agreed, "but don't go further than the park, and be back in time for lunch."

"Thanks, Mum." Rachel said, slipping out of her chair.

Kirsty did the same. "We need a ball," she whispered as they went to get their jackets.

"There's one in the shed, I think," Rachel replied.

The girls found a tennis ball and then set off down the road. Although it was autumn, it was quite a warm day and the sun shone down brightly from a blue sky.

"I hope my Moonstone is safe," India said softly, popping her head out of Kirsty's pocket. "I wonder if there are any goblins guarding it."

"We'll soon find out," Rachel replied, stopping in front of a house with a bright red door. "This is the Palmers' house."

The house was only three doors away from Rachel's home, on the corner of the street. Rachel took the ball out of her pocket, slipped round the corner and tossed it over the fence into the back garden. Then she joined Kirsty and India again in front of the house.

"I'll knock on the door," Rachel said, leading the way up the path.

"Let's hope they're in!" replied Kirsty.

Rachel rang the bell, and they waited for quite a while. Just as the girls and India were starting to give up hope, the door opened.

"Hello, Rachel," beamed Mrs Palmer. "And you must be Kirsty. Rachel told me she was having a friend to stay."

"Hello," Kirsty said politely.

"Sorry to disturb you, Mrs Palmer," Rachel said, "but I'm afraid we just lost our ball over your fence."

Mrs Palmer smiled. "As a matter of fact, I was just sitting in the back garden with Ellie. I didn't see your ball come over, though. Do you want to come and look for it?"

"Yes, please," Rachel replied.

"If you don't mind," added Kirsty.

Mrs Palmer opened the door wide. "Go straight through, girls. I'm just popping upstairs for a minute. Ellie's in her pram on the patio, if you want to say hello." Rachel led Kirsty through the kitchen and out through the back door.

India popped
her head out
of Kirsty's
pocket. "The
Moonstone's
here somewhere,"
she cried happily. "I can feel it!"

"It's a big garden," Kirsty said.

"We better start looking
right away."
She and India
hurried over to the
nearest flowerbed and
began to peer among
the shrubs. Meanwhile,
Rachel went across the patio to say
hello to Ellie. But as she walked
towards the pram with its pretty white
sunshade, Rachel began to shiver.

Suddenly there was a chill in the air.
A loud wail came from the pram.

Ellie had started to cry. Ellie must be feeling the cold, too, Rachel thought. But it was quite warm until a moment ago! Mrs Palmer rushed out of the house and ran over to the pram. "It's very strange, Rachel," she said, as she pushed back the sunshade and bent down to pick up the baby. "Ellie's always had trouble sleeping, but ever since we got this mobile for her pram yesterday, she's been sleeping ever so well." Mrs Palmer frowned, lifting Ellie out from under her lacy blanket.

"Something seems to be upsetting her today though; she's been very restless."

As Mrs Palmer picked Ellie up, the baby stretched out her chubby little hand to grab one of the decorations hanging from the mobile. Rachel looked at it more closely. It was hung with silver stars, yellow suns and pale moons. And then, suddenly, her heart missed a beat, for there, glittering in the middle of the mobile, was a cream-coloured stone which flashed with pink and blue light.

53

The Moonstone! Rachel thought excitedly. *No wonder Ellie's been sleeping well. She must have been having extra-sweet dreams!*

"I'm just going to take Ellie inside," said Mrs Palmer. "There's a chill in the air, all of a sudden."

"I hope that doesn't mean that some of Jack Frost's goblins are nearby," Rachel murmured to herself.

Leaving Mrs Palmer wrapping Ellie in a blanket, Rachel ran down the garden towards Kirsty and India, who were searching round the birdbath in the middle of the lawn.

"I've found the Moonstone!" Rachel whispered triumphantly. "It's hanging in the middle of the mobile on Ellie's pram."

"Wonderful!" India gasped.

"Well done, Rachel!" added Kirsty.

"Mrs Palmer's taking Ellie inside," said Rachel. "We can get the Moonstone as soon as she's gone."

The girls and India watched as Mrs Palmer carried Ellie into the house. Then Rachel and Kirsty immediately ran towards the pram, with India flying along beside them. But before they reached it, the door of the garden shed flew open with a crash, and two green goblins rushed out!

Hot Pursuit!

"The Moonstone is ours!" one of the goblins yelled. "And we'll never let the fairies have it back!"

"Never! Never!" shouted the other goblin.

As Kirsty, Rachel and India watched in horror, he leapt up onto the pram and grabbed at the string on which the

Moonstone was dangling.

"He's going to take the Moonstone!" Rachel gasped. "Stop him!"

As the girls rushed towards the pram, the other goblin panicked.

Hurriedly, he began pushing the pram off the patio, away from the girls. But the pram was much bigger than the goblin, who was only knee-high, and he couldn't control it properly.

It bumped and bounced over the grass and onto the garden path. The goblin inside was caught off-balance.

With a screech of rage, he tumbled over and got caught up in the baby's blankets, before he could grab the Moonstone.

Kirsty, Rachel and India chased after the pram as the goblin charged down the garden path, pushing it in front of him. They could see the Moonstone swinging wildly on the mobile, but they couldn't reach it – the goblins were too far ahead. The pram bounced and jolted its way along, while the goblin inside was struggling to free himself from the tangle of blankets, and he shouted crossly at his friend to stop.

Then, all of a sudden, one wheel hit a large stone lying in the middle of the path. The pram was going so fast that it overturned. Both goblins let out shrill cries of alarm as they flew through the air. And then they both landed in a heap, covered in Ellie's sheets and blankets, underneath a large fir tree.

"India, can you stop
the goblins from
getting away?"
Kirsty panted,
as she and Rachel
chased down
the path towards
the goblins.

"I have a little
dream magic left
which might send the
goblins to sleep," India replied.

She zoomed ahead of the girls and
hovered over the goblins, waving her
wand. A few sparkles of fairy dust
drifted down onto the goblins, who
stopped struggling to free themselves
and began yawning and rubbing their
eyes instead.

"I'm so tired!" one of them sighed.

"And this blanket is really warm and cosy," the other one said sleepily. "I think I might have a little nap."

"Me too," the first goblin agreed. "Sing me a lullaby."

"No, you sing a lullaby!" the second goblin demanded.

"No, YOU!" yelled the first.

"They're waking themselves up with their silly argument!" Rachel exclaimed. "What are we going to do?"

"I think I have an idea!" Kirsty whispered, hurrying towards the goblins.

Rock-a-bye Goblins

Rachel and India watched as Kirsty began to tuck the goblins snugly into the blanket.

"Now, now, settle down," she said in a soft, sweet voice. "It's time for your nap."

The goblins stopped arguing and started yawning again.

"I am sleepy," the first goblin murmured, snuggling down under the pink blanket.

But the second goblin was trying hard to keep his eyes open. "Wasn't there something we were supposed to be doing?" he asked.

Rachel hurried over to help Kirsty. "Go to sleep now," she said in a soothing voice. "You can worry about that later."

And Kirsty began to sing a lullaby to
the tune of *Rock-a-bye Baby:*
"Rock-a-bye Goblins wrapped in a rug,
Asleep in the garden, all nice and snug,
When you wake up from your little nap,
You will find India's got her stone back."

By the second line of
Kirsty's little song,
both goblins were
snoring soundly.

"Well done,
Kirsty," Rachel said
with a grin. "But we
can't leave the goblins
here for Mrs Palmer to find!"

"Leave that to me," India replied. She
waved her wand over a large branch
of the fir tree. Immediately, the branch
drooped lower, so that the leaves

completely covered the sleeping goblins.

"Perfect!" Kirsty declared. "The goblins are green like the leaves, so they'll be well hidden until they wake up."

India and Rachel laughed.

"Then they'll have to rush back to Jack Frost and tell him they've lost the Moonstone," India said. "They'll be in big trouble!"

Chuckling quietly, the girls picked up
the pram and pushed it back to
the patio. Then, as India
watched in delight,
Kirsty carefully
took the magic
Moonstone from
the middle
of the mobile.
It flashed and
gleamed in
the sunlight.

"We mustn't spoil
Ellie's mobile," India said.
She waved her wand and a
glittering, shiny bubble appeared in
place of the Moonstone on the mobile.

As it caught the light, it sent
rainbow-colours shining in all directions.

"And now," India went on, "the Moonstone is going straight back to Fairyland and the Queen's tiara, where it belongs!" She touched her wand to the jewel. Immediately a fountain of sparkling fairy dust shot up into the air and the Moonstone vanished.

"Thank you, girls," India said, giving Rachel and Kirsty a hug. "I must go home now, but I hope you'll be able to help the other Jewel Fairies find their magic stones too."

"We'll do our best!" Rachel promised.

"Goodbye, India!" Kirsty added, as their fairy friend flew away in a cloud of sparkles.

"I wonder where the other six jewels are hiding," Rachel murmured.

"And I wonder if we'll have to face many more goblins," Kirsty said with a frown.

Rachel shivered, remembering her nightmare. "I just hope I don't dream about them again tonight," she said.

Kirsty laughed. "Don't worry, Rachel," she told her friend. "India's got the Moonstone back now; she's sure to send you sweet dreams!"

The Jewel Fairies

India has got her moonstone back.
Now Rachel and Kirsty
must help

Scarlett the Garnet Fairy

Win a Rainbow Magic
Sparkly T-Shirt and Goody Bag!

In every book in the Rainbow Magic Jewel Fairies
series (books 22-28) there is a hidden picture of a jewel with
a secret letter in it. Find all seven letters and
re-arrange them to make a special Fairyland word,
then send it to us. Each month we will put the entries into a
draw and select one winner to receive a
Rainbow Magic Sparkly T-shirt and Goody Bag!

Send your entry on a postcard to Rainbow Magic Jewel
Competition, Orchard Books, 96 Leonard Street,
London EC2A 4XD. Australian readers should
write to Hachette Children's Books, Level 17/207
Kent Street, Sydney, NSW 2000.
Don't forget to include your name and address.
Only one entry per child. Final draw: 30th September 2006.

Coming Soon...
Stella the Star Fairy

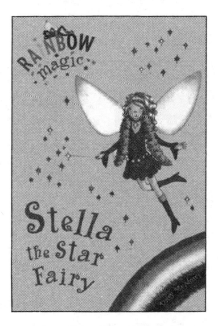

STELLA THE STAR FAIRY

1-84362-869-4

Stella the Star Fairy can't keep Christmas
bright and shiny without her three magical
tree decorations. Can Kirsty and Rachel
help her get them back to the fairy tree
by Christmas Eve, or will the season
be ruined for everyone?

by Daisy Meadows

The Rainbow Fairies

The Weather Fairies

The Party Fairies

The Jewel Fairies

Coming Soon: The Pet Fairies

All priced at £3.99. *Holly the Christmas Fairy, Summer the Holiday Fairy* and *Stella the Star Fairy* are priced at £4.99.
Rainbow Magic books are available from all good bookshops, or can be ordered direct from the publisher: Orchard Books, PO BOX 29, Douglas IM99 1BQ
Credit card orders please telephone 01624 836000
or fax 01624 837033 or visit our Internet site: www.wattspub.co.uk
or e-mail: bookshop@enterprise.net for details.

To order please quote title, author and ISBN and your full name and address.
Cheques and postal orders should be made payable to 'Bookpost plc.'
Postage and packing is FREE within the UK
(overseas customers should add £2.00 per book).
Prices and availability are subject to change.

Have you checked out the

Website at:

www.rainbowmagic.co.uk

There are games, activities and fun things to do, as well as news and information about Rainbow Magic and all of the fairies.